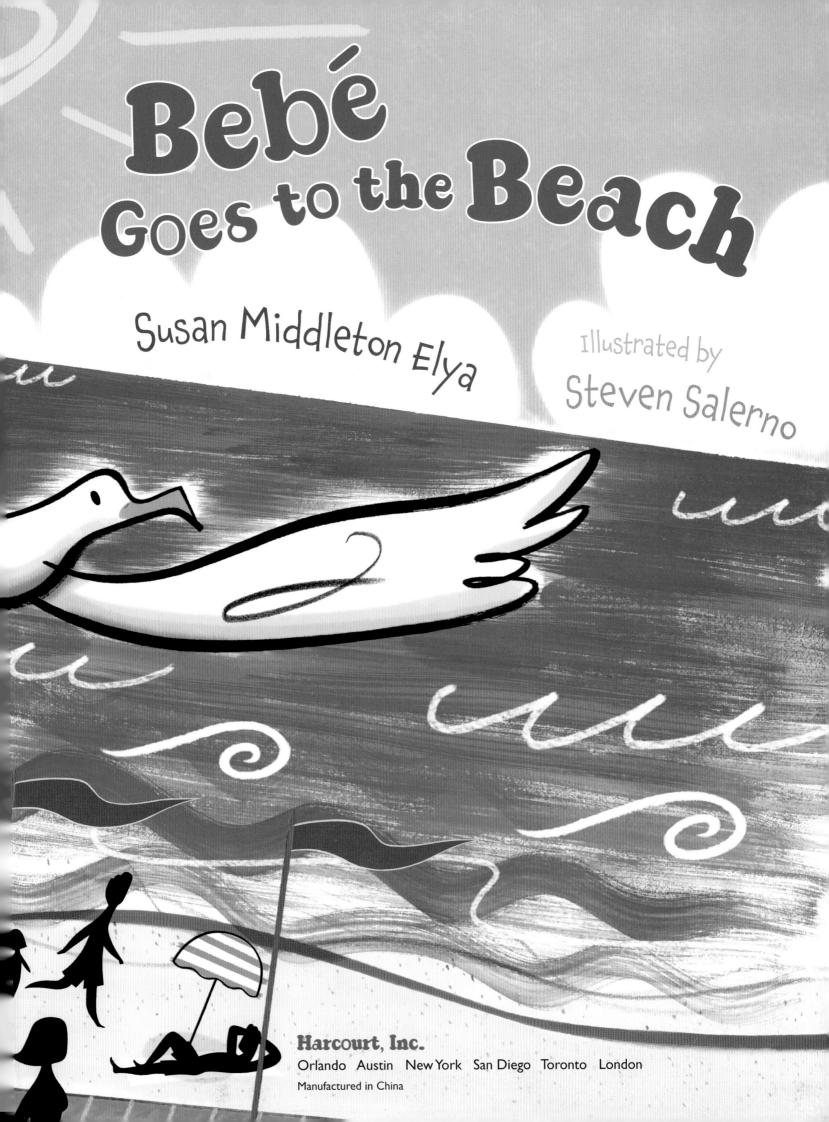

Bebé Goes to the Beach

Susan Middleton Elya

Illustrated by
Steven Salerno

Harcourt, Inc.
Orlando Austin New York San Diego Toronto London
Manufactured in China

A day at the beach! It stretches for miles.
Bebé looks around, all giggles and smiles.

He's wearing his **gorro** with fuzzy **jirafas**.
Mamá parks her **silla** and puts on her **gafas**.

The rolling white **olas** are foamy and loud.
Bebé waddles after them, right through the crowd.

Mamá's coming, too; she remembered the lotion—

he squeals as his toes hit the icy-cold ocean.

"¡**Mira!**" **Mamá** points the way for **Bebé**.

"Let's eat the picnic I packed for today."

There's bread, fruit, and cheese—
pan, **fruta**, **queso**—

and a cupful of juice, served with a **beso**.

Mamá wipes his face, lies back in her chair.
Bebé's on the go, **otra vez**, but to where?

He's zeroing in
on a bouncing **pelota**.

Mamá throws her crumbs to a sly **gaviota**,
then snags **Bebé's** waist, swings him high in the air.
So squirmy! She carries him back to their chair.

Mamá puts him down, set to soak up **el sol**.

Bebé doesn't stay there.
He's ready to roll!

Toddling away, he inspects something **fina**.
Long, golden, slimy, it's **alga marina**!

Bebé tries to bite it.
Mamá yells out,

"¡MALA!"

She grabs it and gives him a bucket and **pala**.
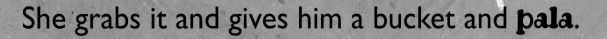

He builds a **montaña**, a valley, a river,
then thinks of **Mamá**, a gift he can give her.

The radio broadcasts **Mamá's** favorite cha-cha,
Bebé dumps the **cub**o of sand on her—gotcha!

"¡**Hijo!**" She grabs him and tickles his tummy.

"Let's get some ice cream. ¡**Sabroso!** So yummy!"

What's that **en la playa**? A tugboat? A turtle?

Bebé climbs a surfboard, not much of a hurdle.

On top of the sculpture, he stretches his **brazos**,

a surfer-dude baby . . .

the board in **pedazos**!

The sculptor runs over, says, "Please, no! **¡Cuidado!**"

Mamá says they're sorry. **Bebé** spies **helado**.

Un hombre is selling both chocolate and **fresa**.
Bebé cannot wait for his creamy **sorpresa**.

He wears **un babero** to catch sticky dribbles.
Mamá sneaks a taste between baby-sized nibbles.

Bebé and **Mamá** wander back, hand in hand,
their footprints both little and big in the sand.

Bebé's eyes are sleepy, his tummy is **llena**,
the towel feels cozy on sunbaked **arena**.

Mamá gets a break now. "At last, **descansaré!**"
But who had the best time of all?

Sweet **Bebé!**

Glossary

alga marina (AHL-gah mah-REE-nah): seaweed

arena (ah-REH-nah): sand

bebé (beh-BEH): baby

beso (BEH-soe): kiss

brazos (BRAH-soce): arms

cubo (KOO-boe): bucket

cuidado (kwee-DAH-doe): careful

descansaré (dehs-kahn-sah-REH): I will rest

el sol (EHL SOLE): the sun

en la playa (EHN LAH PLAH-yah): on the beach

fina (FEE-nah): fine

fresa (FREH-sah): strawberry

fruta (FROO-tah): fruit

gafas (GAH-fahs): glasses

gaviota (gah-VYOE-tah): seagull

gorro (GOE-rroe): small hat

helado (eh-LAH-doe): ice cream

hijo (EE-hoe): son

jirafas (hee-RAH-fahs): giraffes

llena (YEH-nah): full

mala (MAH-lah): bad

mamá (mah-MAH): mom

mira (MEE-rah): look

montaña (mone-TAH-nyah): mountain

olas (OE-lahs): waves

otra vez (OE-trah VEHS): again

pala (PAH-lah): shovel

pan (PAHN): bread

pedazos (peh-DAH-soce): pieces

pelota (peh-LOE-tah): ball

queso (KEH-soe): cheese

sabroso (sah-BROE-soe): tasty

silla (SEE-yah): chair

sorpresa (sohr-PREH-sah): surprise

un babero (OON bah-BEH-roe): a bib

un hombre (OON OME-breh): a man

For Kathleen, sorry about the beach guesthouse;
this will have to do instead.
—S. M. E.

For Samantha, Grady, and their very own new *bebé*!
To all the sunny times they'll have together at the beach.
—S. S.

Text copyright © 2008 by Susan Middleton Elya
Illustrations copyright © 2008 by Steven Salerno

Requests for permission to make copies of any part of the work should be submitted online
at www.harcourt.com/contact or mailed to the following address: Permissions Department,
Harcourt, Inc., 6277 Sea Harbor Drive, Orlando, Florida 32887-6777.

www.HarcourtBooks.com

Library of Congress Cataloging-in-Publication Data
Elya, Susan Middleton, 1955–
Bebé goes to the beach/Susan Middleton Elya; illustrated by Steven Salerno.
p. cm.
Summary: A baby and his mother spend a day at the beach. Spanish words,
interspersed in the rhyming text, are defined in a glossary.
[1. Beaches—Fiction. 2. Mother and child—Fiction. 3. Spanish language—Vocabulary.
4. Stories in rhyme.] I. Salerno, Steven, ill. II. Title.
PZ8.3.E514Beb 2008
[E]—dc22   2006034448
ISBN 978-0-15-206000-8

First edition
A C E G H F D B

The illustrations in this book were done using brushes, colored pencils, gouache,
watercolor, and colored inks on French Arches 260 lb hot pressed
watercolor paper, with added digital color embellishments.
The display type was set in Collins.
The text type was set in GillSans.
Color separations by Bright Arts Ltd., Hong Kong
Manufactured by South China Printing Company, Ltd., China
Production supervision by Pascha Gerlinger
Designed by April Ward